The Red Lantern

by Irma Grant

To Ashley Adajar
Happy New Year
布畾 Carant

Transamerica Pyramid,
San Francisco, California

For Ellie
and Klara,
with love.

Softcover ISBN 978-0-9996033-8-3

This book was typeset in Adobe Garamond Pro

Annie stepped off the cable car.
"Brr! I'm cold," she said, zipping up her coat.

"Come," said Gung Gung. "We are late."

They stopped in front of Gung Gung's Wok Shop. The metal gate creaked as he pushed it aside.

"Stack these," said Gung Gung, pointing to a cardboard box filled with silk paper lanterns. Annie loved spending weekends helping her grandfather, especially around Chinese New Year.

Clay / Sandy Pots
for Stove top

Annie opened the box. She picked up a red lantern and carefully stretched it apart. POOF! A cloud of smoke escaped, revealing a lady in red.

"Who are you?" asked Annie.

"I am the Jade Emperor's daughter."

"Many years ago, I came down from the heavens to warn people about my father's plan to destroy their village with a firestorm. Some hunters had accidentally killed my father's favorite celestial bird and he wanted revenge."
"What did the villagers do?" asked Annie.

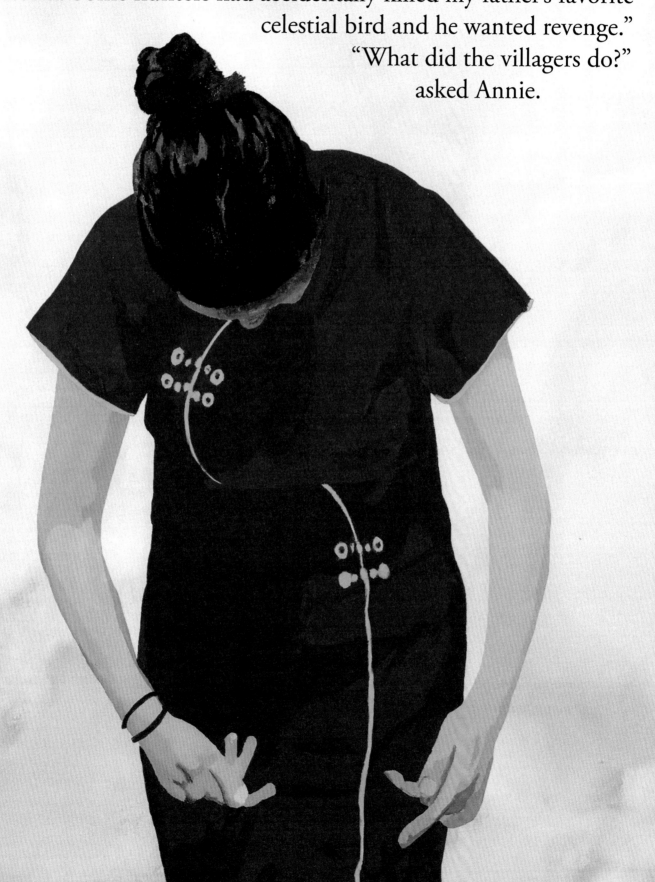

"They hung lanterns, built huge bonfires and displayed magnificent fireworks to trick my father into thinking their town was in flames."
"Did it work?" asked Annie.

"Yes, but my father was angry with me when he figured out what really happened. As punishment, he sends me back to earth each year during the Lantern Festival, when people celebrate the villagers' narrow escape from the firestorm.

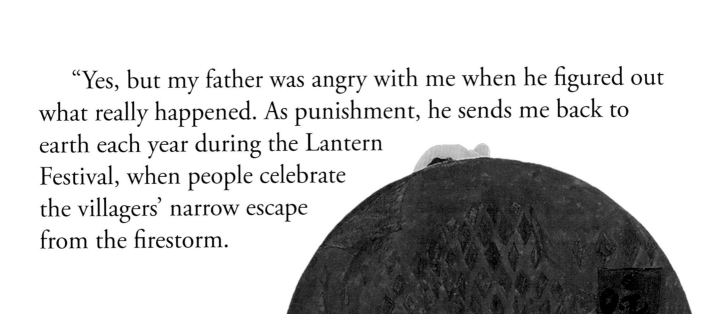

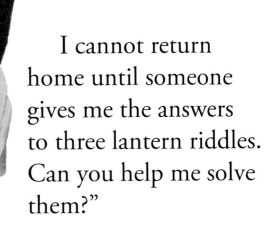

I cannot return home until someone gives me the answers to three lantern riddles. Can you help me solve them?"

I am the perfect summer treat
My outer shell is thick and green
My red insides taste juicy sweet
To eat me is a messy scene

Grandfather emerged from the back of
the store. "Ngoh ho tong ngoh," he said.
"I'm hungry."

For lunch, Annie bought the biggest fruit she could find from Auntie Wo's Produce.

"I figured out the answer to the first riddle," said Annie, "a watermelon!"

"Good thinking! Now here is the second riddle," said the Jade Emperor's daughter.

Two strands of hair upon her head
She wears a most beautiful gown
And dances near a flower bed
The fairest creature in the town

Annie finished stacking the last lanterns onto the shelf.

"Annie," said Gung Gung. "Go buy some plum blossoms for the counter."

"Gong Hay Fat Choy,"
said Annie as she entered Mei Wo Florist.
"Happy New Year."

Annie bought plum
blossoms and a cup of sweet
soup made with sticky rice balls.
    Carrying the steaming tang-yuan in one hand
and the flowers in the other, she hurried back to
grandfather's shop.

"A butterfly," said Annie, "a butterfly!"

"Great! One more and I can go home," said the Jade Emperor's daughter.

> *It follows you a thousand miles*
> *And never wanders far from home*
> *It has no fears and always smiles*
> *At night, it leaves you all alone*

"Annie,"
said Gung Gung
after helping the last customer.
"Let's go to the dragon parade."
Annie skipped across the store, picked up the red
lantern and followed Grandfather out the door.

"Look," said Gung Gung, pointing to the ground. "The sun reminds us that we are never alone."

"My shadow!" said Annie as it disappeared with the setting sun. "That's the answer to the third riddle."

At that same moment, a gust of wind swooped up the red lantern, making it rise higher and higher toward the full moon. The Jade Emperor's daughter was on her way home.

Fire crackers exploded. Red, yellow, and orange streaks lit up the night sky. The city glowed as if on fire.

THE END

Cantonese to English Translations

Gung Gung [gùnggùng] = Grandfather
Ngoh ho tong ngoh [ngóh hóu tóuhngoh] = I'm hungry
Gong hey fat choy [gung hey fah choy] = Happy New Year
Tang-yuan [tāngyuán] = Sweet dumpling balls made of glutinous
    rice flour and bean paste fillings

79971640R00020

Made in the USA
Lexington, KY
27 January 2018